THE BOOK OF TENS

BY MARK PODWAL

GREENWILLOW BOOKS / NEW YORK

FOR
ARIEL

Printed in Singapore by Tien Wah Press
First Edition
10 9 8 7 6 5 4 3 2 1

Library of Congress Cataloging-in-Publication Data
Podwal, Mark H. (date)
The book of tens / by Mark Podwal.
  p.   cm.
ISBN 0-688-12994-3 (trade).   ISBN 0-688-12995-1 (lib. bdg.)
1. Numbers in the Bible—Juvenile literature.   2. Ten (The number)—Juvenile literature.   3. Bible. O.T.—Legends.   4. Midrash—Legends.   5. Jews—Folklore.
I. Title.   BS1199.N85P63   1994   296.1'9—dc20   93-43871   CIP   AC

INTRODUCTION

TEN's practical significance stems from the use of the fingers in counting. Thus, in English the word *digit* refers to a finger or toe as well as a number.

But ten is also endowed with many sacred meanings, especially among the Jewish people. For example, the number ten figures prominently in Jewish worship. Ten individuals comprise a *minyan*, the quorum required for certain religious ceremonies. At the start of each new year, a Jew has ten days in which to pray for God's forgiveness. On Yom Kippur, the Day of Atonement, a legend is recited that tells about ten of Israel's greatest sages, who were martyred by the Romans to "pay" for the sin of Joseph's ten brothers.

Each letter of the Hebrew alphabet stands for a number. The letter *yod* is ten and is the first letter of God's name. When the Holy Temple still stood in Jerusalem, only the High Priest was permitted to pronounce God's name, and only on the tenth day of each year, the Day of Atonement. On that day he would pronounce God's name ten times.

The Torah, the five books of Moses, teaches that the tenth part of anything belongs to God and is holy. The Talmud, the great collection of Jewish ethical and legal writings and legends, teaches that ten symbolizes perfection and completeness. Of the ten measures of beauty that were given to the world, says the Talmud, Jerusalem was granted nine. The Jewish mystics, known as the kabbalists, teach that God governs the world by ten fundamental principles, the *sefirot*.

In Jewish legend and folklore, every creature, every person, every event—all are said to be connected. Pharaoh and the Egyptians suffered ten plagues, one for each of the ten times that Abraham had endured God's trials several hundred years before. Ten Commandments were given to Moses at Mount Sinai, one for each of the ten words that created the world.

Ten appears and reappears so frequently in the holy scriptures that the story of the Bible can almost be retold by means of its citings. What follows are a few of the tales, legends, miracles, and images that recount the Biblical saga of the Jewish people, and all of them involve the number ten.

God had created many worlds before this one. But since none of them pleased Him, He did not let them survive. And so, according to the Talmud, before beginning the creation of the heavens and the earth, God prepared the Torah, paradise, hell, repentance, His throne in heaven, and the celestial Temple.

When He was ready to create this world, He asked the Torah for assistance. The Torah offered Him the help of "twenty-two laborers": the twenty-two letters of the Hebrew alphabet that in their various combinations comprise the holy text.

Using these letters, God formed the ten words He spoke to create the world.

10 words created the world.

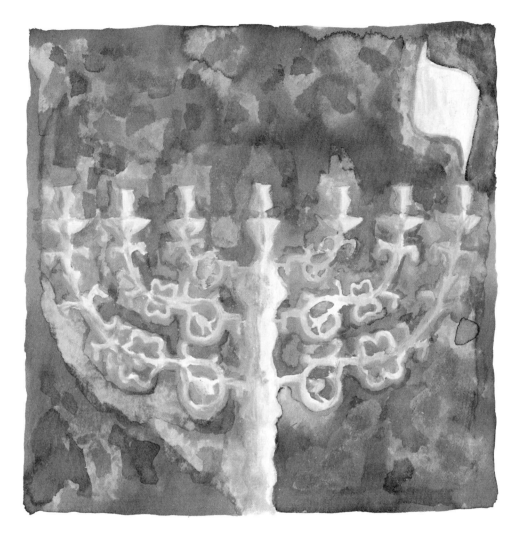

There is a tradition that the seven lights of the *menorah* represent the six days of Creation, with the central light symbolizing the Sabbath, the seventh day, the day of rest.

The ten wonders created on the first day were the heavens and the earth, chaos and emptiness, light and darkness, wind and water, the length of the day, and the length of the night.

10 wonders were created on the first day.

One of the ten reasons traditionally given for the sounding of the *shofar* (ram's horn) on Rosh Hashanah, the Jewish New Year, is that it should serve as a reminder of the ram sacrificed by Abraham in the place of his son Isaac. The ram had been created during the twilight just before the first Sabbath eve and, from that time on, remained in paradise, awaiting the moment to take Isaac's place on the sacrificial altar.

The other marvels created at the same time were the rainbow; Aaron's rod, used to summon forth the ten plagues; the tablets of the Ten Commandments; the stylus God used to engrave the Ten Commandments; manna, the food that fell from the heavens to feed the Children of Israel in the wilderness; Miriam's well that accompanied the Children of Israel in the wilderness; Balaam's donkey's power of speech; the burial place of Moses; and the *shamir*, the worm-like creature that cut the stones used to build King Solomon's Temple in Jerusalem.

10 marvels were created at twilight just before the first Sabbath eve.

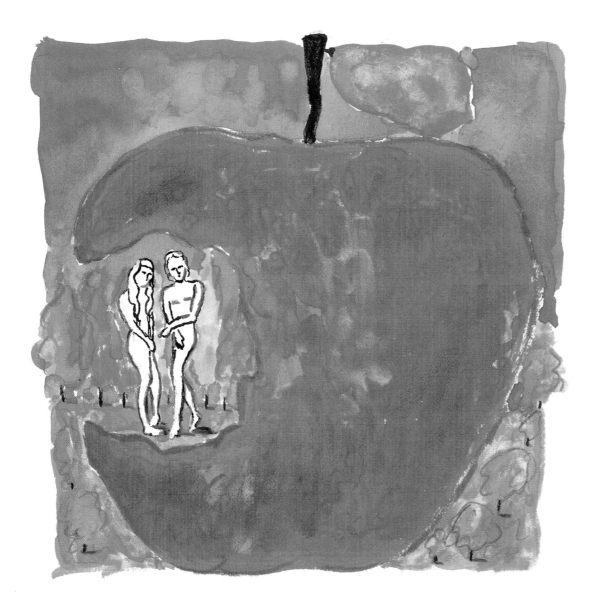

10 curses each were inflicted on the serpent, on Adam and Eve, and on the earth.

Upon learning that Adam and Eve had eaten the forbidden fruit of the tree of knowledge and that the serpent was to blame, God punished each of them with ten curses.

Adam was stripped of his heavenly garments; his food would be the grasses of the field; he was to earn his daily food in sorrow; his children were condemned to wander from land to land; his body would sweat; animals would have the power to kill him; he would no longer live forever; his days would be full of trouble; and in the end he would become dust again and have to answer for all his deeds on earth.

Most severe of the curses that Eve would endure were that she would suffer terrible pain in childbirth and that her husband would be master over her.

Among the serpent's punishments were that its tongue would be split and its hands and feet chopped off.

Because God had instructed the earth to watch over Adam and Eve and the earth had failed to report their misdeed, it too was held accountable. Some of the earth's punishments were that it would have to depend on water from the rain above; sometimes its fruits would fail; it would be divided into mountains and valleys; and one day the earth would grow old.

God spoke to no one in the ten generations between Adam and Noah. The ten generations from the creation of the world to the great flood were represented by Adam, Seth, Enosh, Kenan, Mahalalel, Jared, Enoch, Methusaleh (who lived 969 years), Lamech, and Noah.

After ten more generations, God spoke again, this time to Abraham. The ten generations from Noah to Abraham were represented by Shem, Arpachshad, Shelah, Eber, Peleg, Reu, Serug, Nahor, Terah, and Abraham.

God granted these generations long lives to offer them the chance to show compassion for one another. But they failed to do so.

10 generations passed from Adam to Noah, and **10** more from Noah to Abraham.

In the land of Shinar, King Nimrod began building a colossal tower. Nimrod was one of the ten kings who ruled the earth from one end to the other. When God saw that the tower would be so tall that its top would touch heaven, He came down to earth to put an end to the work. It was one of the ten times God set foot in our world.

Until that time everyone had spoken the same language. But now God gave the people different languages, and since they could no longer understand one another, they were unable to finish the tower. Legend has it that whoever walks on the place where the tower, later known as the Tower of Babel, once stood forgets all he or she ever knew.

10 years after Noah died, the building of the Tower of Babel began.

Abraham's father was a maker and seller of idols. One day while his father was away, Abraham broke every idol in his father's shop, except for the largest one. In this idol's hand he placed an ax. When Abraham's father returned, he demanded to know what had happened. Abraham told him that the biggest idol had killed all the others so he could eat their food. When Abraham's father argued that idols did not eat food and were incapable of doing anything, Abraham asked, "Then why do you worship them?"

Although Abraham had recognized, even as a child, that there was one true God, God tested Abraham's faith ten times. God made him leave the security of his father's house; go to war against kings; suffer hunger, humiliation, imprisonment, and exile; be thrown into a fiery furnace; endure the pain of circumcision at the age of ninety-nine; send away his son Ishmael; and take his son Isaac to be sacrificed.

Without questioning or protesting, Abraham did whatever God asked. And as his reward, God blessed Abraham and promised to make his descendants into a great nation.

10 times was Abraham tested.

When God was deciding whether to destroy the wicked city of Sodom, He came down to earth in another of His ten descents to our world. God wanted to see for Himself if the people of Sodom were as evil as He had heard.

Only when Abraham pleaded on behalf of the city, asking that the good people not be destroyed together with the evil, did God promise to spare Sodom if ten righteous men could be found in the city. But Abraham could not find even so small a number.

So God rained fire and brimstone upon Sodom. He destroyed the people and everything that grew on the ground. And when Sodom no longer existed, the Dead Sea appeared in its place.

10 righteous men could have saved Sodom from destruction.

Isaac had intended to bless Esau, his favorite son, but Rebecca, Isaac's wife, helped her favorite son, Jacob, steal the blessing. She disguised Jacob as his brother so that Isaac, who could not see, would think that Jacob was Esau.

Legend attributes Isaac's blindness to the time he was bound upon the altar, waiting to be sacrificed by his father. The angels wept at the sight, and their tears fell into Isaac's eyes, making him blind.

The ten blessings given to Jacob by Isaac were: May God give you the dew of heaven and the fat of the land, and plenty of grain and wine; nations shall serve you and bow down to you; you shall be master over your brothers, and your mother's sons shall bow to you; a curse on all who curse you, and a blessing on all who bless you.

And God Himself blessed Jacob in a dream in which angels were going up and down a ladder that reached from the ground far into the sky.

10 blessings were given by Isaac to Jacob.

Jacob loved Joseph the most of all his children and made him a splendid coat of many colors, which could be folded into the palm of a hand.

Joseph's brothers were very jealous of him and hated him so much that one day they threw him into a pit full of snakes and scorpions. When a caravan of Ishmaelites passed by, the brothers decided to sell Joseph to the merchants. The Ishmaelites bought Joseph for twenty pieces of silver and took him with them into Egypt, where they sold him into slavery.

All of Joseph's brothers participated in the sale—except Benjamin. And since Benjamin had had nothing to do with the transgression, King Solomon's Temple was built, seven hundred years later, on Mount Moriah, in the territory that belonged to Benjamin's descendants.

10 brothers of Joseph sold him into slavery.

These were the ten plagues that punished Pharaoh and the Egyptians: the turning of all the water in Egypt into blood, including the water in every pitcher and drinking vessel; frogs that covered the whole land; lice; wild beasts; pestilence; boils; hail that knocked down every blade of grass and shattered every tree; locusts that ate all the grass and leaves so that nothing green was left growing in all the land; a darkness so thick that one could touch it; and the slaying of the firstborn sons.

While the Egyptians suffered ten plagues, the Children of Israel experienced ten miracles. These ten miracles were that they were spared the ten plagues.

10 plagues punished Pharaoh and the Egyptians.

10 miracles were performed for the Children of Israel at the Red Sea.

When God blew back the Red Sea with a strong wind, allowing the Children of Israel to pass through safely and escape from the advancing Egyptian army, the waters swelled to a height of sixteen hundred miles and could be seen by all the nations of the earth. Yet the splitting of the sea was only the first of ten miracles witnessed that night by the Children of Israel.

The other miracles were that the waters formed a canopy above their heads; twelve passages opened, one for each of the twelve tribes; the water became as clear as glass so that the tribes could see one another; the ground became dry but turned into mud when the Egyptians tried to cross; the walls of water changed into rocks, against which the Egyptians were thrown, but the rocks crumbled into tiny fragments before the Israelites; a stream of fresh water flowed through the undrinkable salty waters so that the Children of Israel could quench their thirst; and the fresh water then froze and became hidden in the sea after they had finished drinking.

When the Egyptian army saw these miracles, they panicked and tried to flee. But God returned the sea to the way it had always been and hurled the Egyptians into the waters. And all of Pharaoh's army drowned.

Ten laws, one for each of the ten words that created the world, were engraved by God on two tablets. The two tablets, also the work of God's hand, were among the ten wonders created at twilight just before the first Sabbath eve. One legend says that they were formed from a piece of the foundation stone, believed to be the center of the world, that lies on Mount Moriah in Jerusalem. Another says that the tablets were fashioned out of a sapphire from God's throne. Although the tablets were made of stone, they could be rolled up like a scroll.

The rabbis tell us that at first the Children of Israel would not accept God's law. Only after God lifted up Mount Sinai and threatened to drop it on them did the Children of Israel agree to receive His commandments.

The tablets God gave to Moses were weightless and supported themselves. But when Moses came down from Mount Sinai and saw the Children of Israel worshiping the golden calf, all the writing on the tablets flew off. And the tablets became so heavy that Moses dropped them, and they broke.

10 Commandments were received by Moses at Mount Sinai.

Moses sent twelve chieftains, one from each of the twelve tribes, as spies to explore the Promised Land. The twelve men scouted the land for forty days and returned with its fruit. A single cluster of grapes was so large that two of the men had to carry it between them on a pole.

Although they all said that the land flowed with milk and honey, ten of the chieftains gave a false account, reporting that the land was filled with giants and powerful people who lived in large fortified cities. The ten advised against going there. Only two of the chieftains, Joshua and Caleb, recommended completing the journey.

When God saw the people weeping and wanting to go back to Egypt, He condemned them to wander in the wilderness for forty years, one year for each of the forty days that the chieftains spent in the Promised Land. And God told Moses that not one of the Children of Israel who had seen God's wonders in Egypt and in the wilderness and who had been ungrateful would see the Promised Land. Only Joshua and Caleb were allowed to enter the land because they had told the truth.

This episode was one of the ten incidents that tried God's patience in the wilderness.

10 spies falsely reported that the Promised Land was filled with giants.

The ten strings of King David's harp were made from the gut of the ram that had been sacrificed instead of Isaac.

The harp hung over David's bed at night, and opposite the harp was a window that opened to the north. In the middle of the night a wind would blow on the strings, and the harp would play by itself. And all the people of Israel would hear the melody.

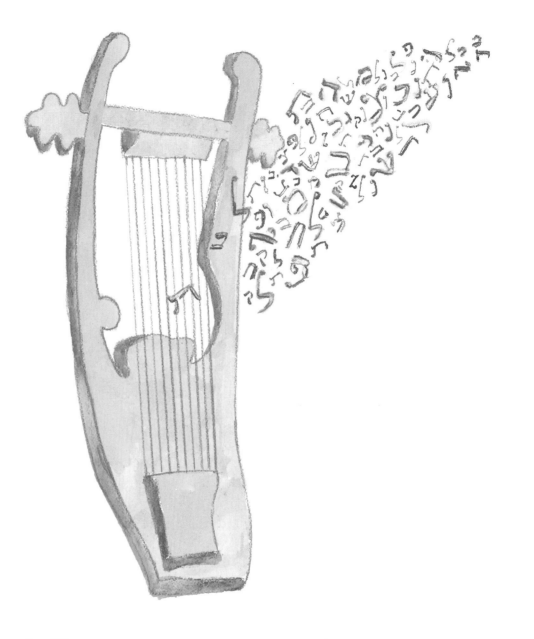

10 strings were made for King David's harp.

10 *menorahs* lit King Solomon's Temple in Jerusalem.

Ten *menorahs* were fashioned from gold for King Solomon's Temple, which stood on Mount Moriah in Jerusalem. It is said that during the seven years it took to build the Temple, none of the workers died, or became ill, or even suffered a tooth-ache. Not a tool used in the work was broken or dented. Indeed, the stones moved on their own and set themselves into the walls.

One of the ten miracles said to have occurred in the Temple was that even when the people stood so close together that no one could force a finger between them, there was still ample space for them to bow down in prayer.

Some say that the dust God used to create Adam was taken from Mount Moriah. It was to Mount Moriah that Abraham came to sacrifice his son Isaac to God.

The rabbis find within the name Moriah the Hebrew word *orah*, meaning "light." When the world was created, according to legend, it was from this mountain that light first shone forth on all the world. And the prophets say that when the Temple, with its ten *menorahs*, stood on this mountain, it too lit up the world.

Perhaps the most beloved of all the prophets is Elijah. Elijah was one of the ten persons permitted to enter heaven in his or her lifetime. He was swept away in a chariot of fire. Among the others who went to heaven without dying first were Abraham's servant Eliezer; Serah, Asher's daughter, who brought Jacob the news that Joseph was alive; and Pharaoh's daughter Bithiah, who saved the infant Moses from the Nile.

10 people went to live in heaven without having died.

History tells us that the ten tribes that constituted the northern kingdom of Israel were banished from their land after their defeat by the Assyrians in 722 B.C.E.

Legend has it that these ten tribes were miraculously carried away into exile beyond the mythical Sabbatyon River. Crossing the Sabbatyon is impossible on weekdays because the river roars with powerful currents overflowing with sand and with rocks as large as houses. Although the river rests on the Sabbath, the laws of that holy day make the river just as impassable then.

So the tribes of Reuben, Simeon, Issachar, Zebulun, Dan, Naphtali, Gad, Asher, Ephraim, and Manasseh continue to live undisturbed to this very day as pious Jews beyond the river. And only when the Messiah comes will the exiles be able to return.

10 tribes were lost in exile.

Daniel was among the Jewish captives who had been carried off to Babylonia after the destruction of King Solomon's Temple in 586 B.C.E. There Daniel predicted that the Persians would overthrow the Babylonian Empire, and they did. King Darius of Persia was so impressed with Daniel's talents that he chose him for prime minister.

The nobles in Darius's court were extremely envious of Daniel. They persuaded Darius to forbid all prayers except those to the king. Because Daniel refused to stop his daily prayers to God, he was thrown into a den with ten famished lions. For six days the lions treated Daniel as faithful dogs would treat their master, wagging their tails and licking him. On the seventh day the den was opened, and all were astonished to see Daniel alive.

When Daniel's enemies proclaimed that Daniel was unharmed because the lions had not been hungry, King Darius ordered the conspirators thrown into the den. The ten lions devoured them immediately.

The king was so moved by the miracle of Daniel's survival that he issued a decree allowing the Jews to return to their land and to rebuild their Temple.

10 lions were in the den with Daniel and did not devour him.

איש
פרשנדתא
דלפון
אספתא
פורתא
אדליא
ארידתא
פרמשתא
אריסי
ארידי
ויזתא

המן למרוד

אסתר וטרים

The Jewish holiday of Purim celebrates with great merriment how the Jews of Persia were saved from the wicked Haman. Read on the evening and the morning of the holiday, the scroll of Esther recounts how Haman, the grand vizier, plotted to kill all the Jews in the Persian Empire. However, the evil plan was foiled by Queen Esther, herself a Jew, and her uncle Mordecai.

Haman was hanged on the very gallows he had built for Mordecai. Also hanged were his sons, whose names were Parshandatha, Dalphon, Aspatha, Poratha, Adalia, Aridatha, Parmashta, Arisai, Aridai, and Vaizatha. It is the custom on Purim, when reading the scroll of Esther, to say all ten names in one breath.

10 sons of Haman were hanged.

A *minyan*, which is required for certain religious ceremonies, consists of at least ten Jews aged 13 years or over. Orthodox Jews count only men in a *minyan*, whereas Conservative and Reform Jews include women.

The number ten was derived from the use of the Hebrew word *edah* ("congregation") in a Biblical verse about the ten spies who gave a false report to Moses about the Promised Land. Some relate the number to the ten righteous men that could have saved Sodom from destruction.

And the Talmud teaches that when ten pray together, God joins them.

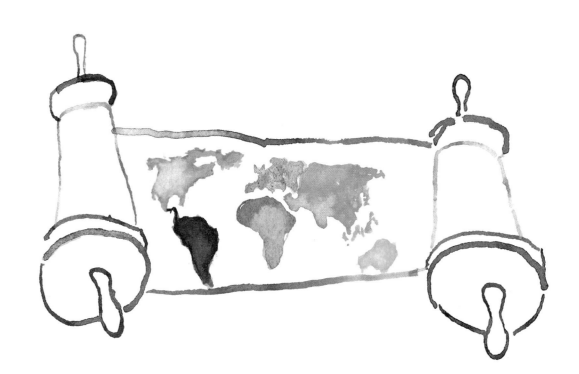

And **10** are needed to come together in a *minyan* to bless God, who can create a world with **10** words.